T0064564

A Very Resilient Amreeki Dream

A Very Resilient Amreeki Dream

Almas Akhtar

authorHOUSE®

AuthorHouse™
1663 Liberty Drive
Bloomington, IN 47403
www.authorhouse.com
Phone: 1 (800) 839-8640

Published by AuthorHouse 05/29/2015

ISBN: 978-1-5049-0740-8 (sc)
ISBN: 978-1-5049-0739-2 (e)

Library of Congress Control Number: 2015905828

Print information available on the last page.

To my parents, for all their love! To my three kids, Allana, Ammar, and Amber, who are my pride and joy! To Yahya, who made me believe in the power of prayers, and especially to my husband, Adil, for giving me all the love and confidence I have today. And to women who are victims of domestic abuse. To all the immigrants who came to the United States of America in search of their dreams, this is for you!

August 2012,
Southfield, Michigan

"It's been two years, and you still can't make tea properly—like my mom used to make. I wonder how many more years I will have to drink this medicated hot water," Asim said.

"I left the tea bag in it for at least four minutes and also warmed the milk before adding it to the tea. I tried, but I can make new one," replied Safina in a very annoyed, somewhat scared tone.

"No, I have to go. I don't need another cup of Joshanda," Asim said as he got up.

Safina picked it up and sniffed it. To her, it did not smell that bad, like the herbal medicine her mother used to make for a sore throat.

"What should I cook for dinner? *Karahi* chicken or *qeema*?" Safina asked, coming near him.

"Don't ask me that. Use your brain—I think you have one!" he laughed.

"Okay. *Khuda Hafiz*," she added, meaning "may God protect you."

Safina tried to give Asim a hug, but he simply rushed out the door. She went to the freezer and took out a frozen bag of minced meat. She knew he always preferred minced beef curry over chicken.

When will I win my husband's heart? When will he actually enjoy talking to me rather than just criticizing me? These thoughts came to her mind every day and every night. *Oh, but he gets tired at work, and he is not a very expressive type of person. I'm sure he loves me in his heart;*

after all, I am his wife. Safina assured herself and simply drained all the negative feelings out of her mind.

She cleared the breakfast dishes from the kitchen table in their ninth-floor Sterling Heights apartment. It was a beautiful summer afternoon. She looked at the trees outside her window. *Soon the colors will change and it will be fall*, she thought. She loved the fall in Michigan; the beautiful colors of orange, maroon, rust, and dark green looked spectacular. She loved this season, but dreaded the cold winter months that followed. She hated winter and was still not adjusted to it even after living in Michigan for twenty-five months. It was the complete opposite of Karachi's warm climate.

Asim and Safina got married in January 2010, and she came to the United States in August of that year. Asim left a few days after the *valima* ceremony, the dinner given by the groom a couple of days after the wedding ceremony. She had to wait a few months for her new passport, and he had to send her H2 visa from his employer. Her in-laws

and parents also wanted her to stay in Karachi so she could enjoy all the many other festivities after the actual wedding. Weddings in Pakistan are quite elaborate and somewhat tiring activities. The wedding ceremony, henna ceremony, and *valima* reception are followed by many dinner parties that close friends and relatives throw in honor of the newly married couple. It is expected that the bride will wear beautiful formal dresses and jewelry at all the parties. That is the reason that the bride has to shop for not only the wedding dress but several more formal outfits before the wedding.

Safina was a simple girl who never rebelled against the ritual of arranged marriages. Unlike many other modern Desi girls, she believed that the person selected by her parents to be her husband would be her true soul mate. He would love her and take care of her. And Asim's behavior was somewhat nice to her in those few initial days—or maybe she did not notice anything amiss. She was just too happy to feel any negativity.

November 2009, Karachi

Asim's mother had short-listed two girls over the course of almost a year after considering many for her younger son.

"You will have to get married this year. I have selected two very pretty girls for you to choose between. You are twenty-eight years old; how many more years can you wait?" said Mrs. Khan.

"*Ami* (mom), I also want some brains with all the beauty," Asim replied.

"All girls become what their husbands want them to be. Your wife will also become what you want her to be. After all, I was only seventeen when I married. Did I not raise five kids, take care of you guys and the house when

your dad was in Dubai, and most of all deal with my meddling in-laws all the time?" she said.

"Yes, *Ami*, okay, okay. But no one can be like you, my *Ami* the great," he said, laughing.

She smiled; he had made her day—or maybe her entire week. "Oh, I love you, my dear Asim. Let's hope you don't forget your mom after your wedding."

Asim was the baby of the family; he had three older sisters and one older brother. Asim was the most educated person in their family. He was a lab technician working at a private pharmaceutical lab in Michigan. He studied in Karachi, and then studied for another year in Michigan, followed by a few months of training. His older brother, Hassan, was not a good student, and instead got involved in the fabric business at an early age. Now he owned a fabric store in the Bohri Bazaar in Karachi. He lived in a three-bedroom apartment in the Saddar, a suburb, with his mother, his wife, and their two sons; they were a blue-collar, middle-class family. All Asim's sisters got

married in their early- to mid-twenties after getting their undergraduate degrees. His younger sister, who had a degree in finance, worked at a bank.

Their father, Feroz Khan, was a construction worker in Dubai who worked day and night to support his wife, children, parents, and two sisters. Mr. Khan was in his early thirties when he got a job in Dubai. He came once a year during Ramadan to Karachi, when he enjoyed time with his family.

His wife sent pictures of the children and letters to him regularly. He called once a week and talked to everyone, even baby Asim, who was only one when he left. His wife cried a lot when he left for Dubai, but he promised her he would come back after five years. Those five years turned into ten, then twenty, and eventually twenty-five. He collected money first for his sisters' marriages and then his own; to buy an apartment; for his parents' medical bills; for his children's education; and at last for his own daughters' weddings. By the time he got done with all his responsibilities, he realized

he was fifty-five years old and a heart patient. Maybe living away from his family, not watching his diet properly, and feeling lonely and homesick took a toll on his health. He took medicines for high blood pressure and had had an angioplasty a few years back, but he still suffered a major heart attack and died on the spot. His body was sent to Pakistan. After his death, Asim, who was twenty-six then, was hired by one of Feroz's friends in the United States who arranged for his visa. Asim already had a degree in pharmacology and studied for another year after moving to United States.

"Feroz took care of everyone. *Mashallah* [God willed it], all three daughters and the older son are happily married, and Asim is done with his studies," said Uncle Alim, Asim's family's neighbor and good friend, on the day of his father's funeral.

But I don't remember having my father at home with us all the time like everyone else. He sent racecars, a boom box, and a motorcycle for me, but I don't remember him taking us to school every day, thought Asim, wiping tears from his face. Since

Asim was very young when his father moved abroad, he only saw his parents living together for a few weeks every year. This left a deep mark on his personality. Asim had seen his mother living alone most of her life while his father was in another country. He felt great pain for her. He was also somewhat angry at the world that if his mother could not spend quality family life with her husband then no one should, no other woman should.

Safina was the oldest of four sisters. She was pretty, with *gori* (fair) skin. People in the subcontinent are still fascinated by a fair complexion; it is a huge advantage for a girl, especially during the process of arranged marriages, since 90 percent of the mothers looking for suitable matches for their sons opt for a fair-skinned girl. She was Asim's sister Humaira's neighbor, and Mrs. Khan really wanted Asim to marry her. Safina's father, Mr. Fazalullah, was a college teacher while her mother, Asia Bibi, was the head of the philosophy department at Karachi University.

She had completed her B.A. Her family highly valued good education, and they wanted her to study more yet did not want to send away good proposals. Her family was somewhat comfortable middle-class family. Her mother, Asia Bibi, was always worried about her four daughters and their marriages. When Humaira said that she would bring her brother to meet Safina the next Saturday, Asia Bibi could not contain her happiness. She prayed that Asim would like Safina so she could marry him and go to "Amreeka," as the Desis call America.

December 2009, Karachi

"*Ami*, its fine I will marry the girl who Humaira Apa's neighbor. But of course it's up to you," Asim finally agreed.

"I will call them tomorrow! Even I like her better than the other girl," replied his mother, beaming with excitement.

Asim frowned and said, "But Ami, I have to ask why you did not visit my friend Farooq's house to meet his sister who is an engineer. "They would have married her to me." He sounded a bit frustrated.

"Asim, I told you I would not go to a big bungalow or to a rich person's house to ask their daughter's hand for you. We are middle-class people who live in a small apartment; we want daughters-in-laws like us. Also, girls

who are too educated are very proud—they think too much of themselves," Mrs. Khan answered in a very firm, rather angry, tone.

Safina and Asim were married on New Year's Eve, 2009, as Asim had to leave for America on January 5. Their wedding was a simple affair by Karachi standards. It was held at a local wedding garden and attended by 250 people. The bride looked very pretty in her pink *sharara*, the long skirt and a long shirt, both heavily embroidered with golden-colored threadwork, and beautiful gold earrings, a necklace, bangles, and of course a *tikka* on her forehead. Twenty-four-carat-gold jewelry is given to the bride by both her family and the groom's family; as a precious metal, its price appreciates with time, so buying jewelry is considered a type of investment in Asian and Arab countries.

At least she is good looking, thought Asim.

He told Safina very bluntly the next morning, "You are my mom's choice. I will try to be a good husband, but I am a very moody person. You will have to learn a lot of things when you come to the US. I guess I will have to teach you everything, like I would a little kid," he said in somewhat a sarcastic tone.

Safina just nodded. *I will learn everything! The English language, driving a car, grocery shopping, and cooking his favorite food*, she thought.

She was a typical Pakistani girl: shy, confused. She had just met her future husband only once for few minutes before her arranged wedding. Theirs was a completely arranged marriage where families decide who the kids should marry and then set up a date, invite friends, do lots of shopping, and make two strangers partners for the rest of their lives. This formula works most of the time, especially if the girl tries to be a good wife, a good daughter-in-law, and later, a good mother. In a way, her

parents were happy that she would be going to Amreeka so that she would not have to deal with her in-laws all the time.

As for Safina, she was happy that she had fallen in love for the first time with the man who was her husband. Maybe it was just the concept of getting married to someone that made her feel that she had fallen in love. She was a little scared but did not show it to anyone. She was a strong girl who believed in the power of true love.

"Please call me as soon as you can. I don't want to live here without you," she said to Asim on the morning of January 5 as he was getting ready to go to the airport.

"It will take at least four to five months, and that is very quick; some girls wait for four to five years till they get their visas. Enjoy your time with my family and yours, since it will be two or three years till you come back to Karachi," he said.

"I just want to be with you." She was holding his hand and crying.

"Look, you are a married woman now! Don't cry. What will everyone think?" Asim said.

"What will they think? That a wife loves her husband and doesn't want him to leave," she said, looking in his eyes.

"Well there is no such thing as love in arranged marriages. It's just a verbal agreement and lots of hard work till we both get old. Life is tough, Safina," Asim said, like a school teacher explaining an algebra problem rather than a newly married husband talking to his new wife.

It took seven months for all the papers to arrive. Safina arrived at Detroit Metro Airport on August 18, 2010.

August 2010,
Sterling Heights, Michigan

Safina was very scared. It was the first time she was going to be on an airplane. She had been on a train many times, but never on an airplane.

Her mother and sisters cried at the airport. "*Ami*, I will be fine," Safina said. She was sad to leave them but very excited to start her new life with Asim, and most of all to see him after almost eight months.

She sat with an older couple on the plane. She was nervous but did not show it to anyone; instead, she looked around and learned quickly what to do and what not to do while on an airplane, like fastening her seatbelt, turning on and off the light switch, and watching in-flight movies.

Asim was waiting at the airport. She blushed when she looked at him. She felt no less than Cleopatra when he hugged her. Then she looked at the newly built Metro Airport with awe and wondered at how big and how beautiful this country was. She had just seen pictures of America, and now she as actually there. She wanted to show Asim her excitement but acted mature in front of him.

"This is your car? It's so cool!" She was very happy to be with him.

"Of course it is mine. It's a little old but in good condition. And yes, it is cool—everything I own is cool, because I have worked very hard for it. This is the United States, my dear, where you have to work day and night to have a decent lifestyle," he replied. Again he sounded like a teacher explaining a difficult problem to a student—or maybe he sounded like an accomplished young man who was proud of himself. "Now I have to go back to work. Hurry up; I will drop you at home, but I will try to come

back early," he said as he put her suitcase in his blue Honda Accord.

"You will drop me there? I thought you would take the day off," she said.

"And who will work and pay the bills?" he snapped.

When they reached the house, he showed her around. "I will come home by six. There is food in the fridge. Don't get scared; watch TV or rest. Oh, and don't turn on the stove—just use the microwave." He gave all the instructions and was about to leave when she came near him and gave him a hug.

"Did you miss me?" she asked affectionately.

"Yes, yes … but I have to go. I will see you in few hours." He smiled somewhat.

Asim does care for me, she thought, and jumped with excitement. *This is my house—no, it's* our *house.* She was touching everything in that tiny apartment: the TV, pots and pans, the basket of mail, the old leather couch, the small wooden coffee table, and the white floor lamp.

Her family's house in Karachi was much bigger than this apartment. Yet she felt that this apartment and the things in it were hers—hers and Asim's—theirs, like they were made for each other. Life was just too perfect, too beautiful for her right now.

December 2010, Chicago

"This is my wife, Safina," Asim said. "Safina, this is Azar, my dear friend." Asim was very excited to see Azar after two years. He had brought Safina to Chicago for a so-called honeymoon, and also to spend time with his friend.

"*Salams*," Safina said, offering the traditional greeting. "How are you?"

"Fatima, where are you? Our guests are here," Azar called. Then, "Here she comes," he said when she came downstairs.

Fatima was a pretty-looking girl in her late twenties who was doing her fellowship at a local hospital and was mother of two-year-old Sasha. "Salams. It's so nice to

finally meet you, Safina! So you are the lucky lady who is the center of affection of Asim Bhai," she said, hugging Safina.

"She is not the center of affection—or as a matter of fact, center of anything. She is just a wife," Asim replied with his usual sarcasm.

Safina got a bit uncomfortable. *Why does he have to say things like this in front of others? Why can't he be a little considerate? Just a little.*

Azar said, "Come on, at least show some affection! After all, you are on your honeymoon in our house in the beautiful city of Chicago on this chilly night."

Safina had always dreamt of a romantic honeymoon, but Asim said he did not believe in honeymoons or Valentine's Day. "I can take you to Chicago during Christmas break. You can meet my friend Azar and his wife. We can stay in a hotel near Lake Shore Drive, and I can take you to Devon Street for *halwa puri* for breakfast." She got excited, because she had been craving the sweet

fried bread very popular back home. "Then we can drive around downtown Chicago at night. It's very beautiful, and they have all the big stores there—Saks, Neiman Marcus, Macy's—but they are too expensive. I don't know anyone who shops there," he said.

Like any new immigrant, Safina wanted to visit all the big US cities like New York, Los Angeles, and Chicago with Asim. They would walk on the streets holding hands and looking at buildings and lakes. But now he wanted them to go to Chicago to meet his friend rather than spend time together with each other. In the end she compromised once again, and got somewhat excited at the thought of going on vacation for a couple of days.

"Safina, Fatima is a physician, a full-time mother, and a gracious host. She is a superwoman. By the way, Azar, you won the lottery," Asim said.

"By the way, I cook, clean, change diapers, and tolerate my wife's many mood swings," replied Azar, laughing.

It was clear Asim was impressed by Fatima. After all, she was earning more than her husband. She was training to become a physician, and physicians earned more than lab techs. Maybe that was why Asim was impressed by her.

The four-day trip was not that bad after all. They ate breakfast on Devon Street; Asim's favorite beef stew, called *nihari, a*nd her favorite *halwa puri* everyday. He took her to all the department stores on Michigan Avenue, but made it clear that they were there to look and not to buy. Safina was fine with that; she just took pictures on her cell phone as souvenirs of their first vacation together.

She really liked a pink sweater, but the price tag said $200, and she had only $85 in her wallet. *Asim will think it is stupidity to spend $200 on a sweater. And who cares about material things? It's the good memories that we should care about*, Safina thought, and put the sweater back. *Some other day.*

September 2012, Sterling Heights

"I will pick you up at 10:00 to take you to the doctor, then I will drop you and go back," Asim said on the phone.

"I can go by myself. It's not that far," she replied.

"You are not going to a grocery store; you are going to see a gynecologist. Which language you will talk in, Urdu?" he said very angrily.

"Asim, I can talk in English. After all, I go to grocery stores, the post office, and the gas station by myself." *Why does he have to find faults in me?* she wondered.

"I don't want you to talk in a funny accent with the doctor. I will come. End of discussion," he said in his rude, authoritative tone.

Asim and Safina were expecting their first baby. She was feeling fine. According to her own calculations, she was almost seven weeks pregnant, so the baby was due in early spring. When she told Asim about the pregnancy after taking the home pregnancy test, he seemed happy at the news but quickly told Safina that he thought women exaggerated their condition during pregnancies. It was not a very tough task, in his mind.

Actually, Asim believed he should be tough with his wife; otherwise, she would start dominating him. Asim had quite a complicated personality. He thought that because she was not very highly educated, had not attended the most top-notch English school in Karachi, and had not lived in an upscale neighborhood that she would never be able to adjust properly in the United States.

Safina wondered when he would respect her and trust her. After all, she had been living in this country for two years by that point. She had learned to drive, mail the monthly bills, do grocery shopping, and complete all the other chores around the house. She had also made friends in the apartment building: a Chinese lady, Mrs. Yang; an Indian couple, the Guptas; and two older *Gora*, or white, couples, the Robinsons and the Kendalls. Her English had improved a lot, and she seemed more relaxed and confident when she was on her own without him.

She thought "America is rightfully called the melting pot because there are people from everywhere around the world, they have totally different cultures, different customs and different languages but when they come to America, they live together in one neighborhood, in one city with peace and harmony, there are not Muslims or Hindus, Christians or Jewish – they are all just human beings helping each other like a big huge family".

"People are very helpful and nice here and make immigrants very comfortable—at least that is my experience," she murmured to herself after he left.

Safina enjoyed taking care of her house and her husband. She cooked all of his favorite dishes, but he rarely appreciated her. "You can never be as good as my mom," he had told her numerous times.

"I don't want to be as good as she is. She is your mom! I just want to be good," she'd reply.

Since Asim had never seen his mother and father living together, he did not know how to behave with a wife. *Or maybe he thinks that only girls who are earning a good salary are good wives*, she thought. *He cares more about money than relationships.*

April 2013,
Southfield, Michigan

March and April were two special months for Asim and Safina. They welcomed their beautiful daughter Anaya Khan in March, and in April they got their green cards.

Safina had a difficult delivery and had to have a C-section. Asim was sweet to her for a few hours immediately after the baby was born—he always wanted a girl. He hugged her after she came to the room. But the affection lasted only a few hours; then he was himself again.

"Everyone—my mom, my sisters—think that Anaya looks like me," Safina said, looking adoringly at her daughter. She had emailed everyone pictures of the baby.

"I hope she studies and become a doctor or engineer. A proper degree-holder, unlike her mother," Asim said.

"Asim, I can study too. After a few years, I can take evening classes," Safina said nervously.

"You will study!" He laughed. "How will you study in this country? People who have not studied in a decent English-medium school in Pakistan don't get admitted to college here."

Safina just stayed quiet; she did not want to get him angry. His words made her very depressed. *I try so hard, but he does not respect me*, she thought sadly.

Safina had a strong personality. She believed in the power of love, that love conquers all.

She had seen her mother rudely dominating her father, who was a little less educated than his wife. He worked at a local college while she was working at the largest University

in town. He always tried to please her mother but could not succeed. Her father's personality shattered due to this fact; he suffered from mild depression. Safina and her sister felt their father's pain. Because of that, Safina thought she would have a good relationship with her husband. She wanted to raise her kids in a happy and healthy environment. Maybe this was the reason she did not fight with Asim.

Asim had never hit her or physically abused her, but he had never, ever respected her. He was great at verbally abusing her. There was some kind of anger he had in his head. He was also very controlling, checking all the bills and grocery receipts. He made a decent salary of $60,000 a year, but only gave her $200 spending money every month. She used it to buy some makeup, clothes, or shoes for herself. Asim did not believe in celebrating wedding anniversaries or birthdays, but she did; she always bought him a card or a small gift. Physical abuse is easily identified. Verbal abuse is different. The pain is internal, there are no physical bruises or scars, just a badly wounded spirit.

April 2013, Southfield

Her neighbor, Mrs. Gupta, called Safina after Asim left for work. "I have some guests coming over on the weekend. Can you make some chicken *biryani* for me? I know you are busy with the baby, but I would really appreciate it! I will pay you for it, of course."

"Oh, I will, Mrs. Gupta. I cook for us too, so don't worry." She couldn't say no to her. Mrs. Gupta had helped her a lot during her pregnancy and in the first week after the baby was born.

"This biryani looks delicious," Mrs. Gupta said, smiling, when she came to pick it up on Friday morning. She opened the cover of the platter and looked at the

popular South Asian dish, a rice and meat mixture sprinkled with green chilies and fried onions. "How much did everything cost?"

Safina replied, "Just twenty-five dollars."

"Okay. You keep this." Mrs. Gupta handed Safina a fifty-dollar bill.

"Let me get change for you." Safina turned to get her bag from her bedroom.

"No, it's for you, for your hard work. Desi restaurants charge $80 for biryani trays this big," Mrs. Gupta said.

"But it was my pleasure! I am not doing a business deal."

"You deserve this. You took time out for me; you worked hard. You can't say no!" Mrs. Gupta left the apartment and Safina looked at the money, somewhat confused.

Mrs. Gupta called the next day. "Safina, my friends loved the biryani. Thank you, thank you so much! You

know, I throw a lot of parties, and I work nine to five. I have never enjoyed cooking my entire life. Is it possible that you could cook for me on a regular basis? You are home with the baby, you can earn some money, and most of all, you are an amazing cook."

"I would be interested, but let me ask Asim," Safina replied.

That evening when Asim came back from the office, she gathered some courage and asked him. "Asim, is it okay if I cook some Pakistani dishes for Mrs. Gupta sometimes? She will pay me; she will in fact pay a little more than what my cost will be. I can do it in the morning when Anaya is asleep!"

"Did she ask you?" he said.

"Yes. She likes my cooking." Safina got a bit excited.

He replied, "It's okay, but do keep track of all expenses. Don't undercharge her; I know they both earn a lot."

Safina never thought that he would give permission to her so easily. She got up and gave him a hug. "Oh, thank you, Asim! You are the best!"

"Well, what else can you do besides cooking? That is the only thing you can do," he said, insulting her again.

But she did not care. She was very happy.

December 2013, Southfield

It had been almost eight months since Safina started her catering business. She was not only cooking for Mrs. Gupta but also for her sister and one of her friends who lived nearby. She made a proper menu card with prices. She was a hard worker, doing all the work in the morning while the baby was taking a nap or sitting in her bouncer. She also enjoyed taking care of the house and playing with Anaya.

Asim's attitude toward her did not change even after the birth of their baby, but Safina was able to divert her attention to her baby and did not care much about his attitude. Her catering business had given her a sort of confidence that she could do something to earn money.

She was making between $500 and $600 a month, and she saved most of it. She spent some of it to buy dresses and toys for the baby. She also bought a small diamond necklace for her younger sister who was getting married and sent it to Karachi with a friend. She knew Asim would have never let her buy an expensive gift for her sister. In fact, he had never bought any gift for his own wife. When her sister called and told her that she really liked it, Safina got extremely happy. These were the tiny pleasures of life that made her happy—actually, that would make anyone happy.

Safina wanted to save money so she could enroll herself in the Montessori Teacher Training course. The wife of one of Asim's friends was doing it, so Safina searched about it online. One could get a diploma in a year through an online course. The certificate holder could get a job at a Montessori school and could earn between $24,000 and $30,000 a year. There were many Montessori schools in

Oakland County, where Safina and Asim lived; they ran from pre-K to third or fourth grade.

It was a cold December evening. The roads were very slippery after a snowstorm. It was about 7:00 p.m. Safina had put the baby down for a nap and was putting the clothes in the washing machine when suddenly her cell phone rang.

"Hello, is this Mrs. Khan?" someone asked in a heavy southern accent.

"Yes, this is she," she replied in a confused and somewhat scared tone.

"We wanted to inform you that your husband was involved in a road accident. We are taking him to Henry Ford Medical Center; you can come there."

"Oh my God, is he okay? Oh, Allah! I am coming!" Tears started to flow from her eyes. "Please God, give my husband health! Help us, please!" She was crying and shaking.

After few minutes, Safina gathered her strength and called Mrs. Gupta with trembling hands to ask her for a ride to the hospital.

"Sure. Both Raj and I will be there in five minutes. Don't worry; Asim will be fine. Bhagwan will take care of him. Put baby's stuff in a bag; we can leave her with Mrs. Yang for a few hours," Mrs. Gupta said, trying to calm Safina.

When she reached the hospital with the Guptas, she was shivering and crying. She wiped her tears when she entered the room Asim was in. They had put in an IV and given him some painkillers, so he was a bit drowsy.

"How are you, dear?" she asked, stroking his cheek.

"I have pain in my leg. The road was slippery," he said.

The doctors took her outside and explained that he had fractured one of his legs and had gotten a few bruises, but otherwise everything was okay. He would hopefully have a full recovery.

"God saved his life. The roads are really bad outside, and his car was in very bad shape when the emergency dispatchers reached the scene of the accident," said the doctor.

"Thank you." She wiped her tears and gathered all her confidence. *I have to be calm and composed so I can take care of my husband.*

"They will keep him for at least a week, then he'll do another two to three weeks at rehabilitation. He will be fine in a month," said Mr. Gupta when she went back inside Asim's room.

"We are here; we all are with you," added Mrs. Gupta as she hugged Safina.

Safina was very worried. She felt lonely all of a sudden. She wondered why this accident did not happen in Karachi, where they had family to help!

"Do you have your insurance card?" someone asked.

She took out the card from her wallet and gave it to the nurse, her hands—her entire body—shaking.

Mrs. Gupta got water for her. "I just called Mrs. Yang. Anaya is fine playing with her kids."

"Okay, thanks," Safina said as she sat on a chair.

She signed some papers and left after a few hours when Asim was asleep. She picked up Anaya from the Yang apartment; the baby was asleep. But Safina could not sleep. All night she prayed, she cried, she turned the TV on and off. She called the hospital several times, and the nurses assured her that her husband was sleeping. They had put a cast on his leg.

She thanked God again and again for saving Asim's life. She had gathered all her strength and was being very strong.

She thought about calling her family in Karachi and tell them about Asim's accident but didn't. *No, I should not worry them. They can't come here anyway,* she thought.

The next morning Safina got ready, left the baby with Mrs. Gupta, and went to see Asim.

He was up but still groggy due to all the pain medication. She sat near the bed holding his hands, and he did not even try to take them away. Maybe he was scared too.

"Where is the baby?" he asked.

"At the Gupta house," she replied. Tears rolled down her cheeks as she said, "Oh, Asim, thank God you are safe!"

"Yeah, thank God. The roads were pretty bad. I just remember seeing a truck. But I will be fine. Don't cry; everyone will see you."

Safina stood up. "Let them see. I am worried for you."

"I am okay. But I am worried; please tell me, did you sign the papers? Did they ask you any questions?" Asim wanted all the details.

"They asked me to sign papers only the first day, just the usual paperwork and insurance info," she replied.

"Okay. Since I am better today, if they ask any other questions, ask them to check with me. You will not be

able to understand all the details in what little English you can speak and understand." *Now he sounds like the typical Asim*, she thought. She wanted to say something but kept quiet; she did not want him to get angrier.

He stayed five days in the hospital and another ten in rehabilitation. She visited him daily, leaving the baby with neighbors. Everyone at Asim's office—his colleagues, their wives— everyone helped her during this tough time. She missed her family in Karachi but was so happy to have found all these wonderful people, especially since the accident had made Asim angrier and much meaner— rather cruel, in fact.

Everyone praised her for taking care of her husband, but not Asim; he just thought it was her duty to take care of him. The hospital was a thirty-minute drive from their house, but the rehab center was closer. That helped, since Safina would cook, clean, and do the grocery shopping in the evening after coming back from the hospital.

Asim came back home after fifteen days. He hugged Anaya for a very long time. Safina got happy. *At least he loves our daughter dearly!*

Asim's best friend, Azar, visited them from Chicago once Asim was home.

"You did not bring Fatima?" Safina asked him.

"She has gone to Los Angles on vacation with her friends," he replied. "She sees me everyday; now she wants to relax and enjoy her friends without a husband in tow." It seemed that he wasn't very happy.

Safina was surprised women could be like that too— could have some "me time" to relax with their friends.

"You know, Asim, your wife is very caring. The most important thing is that you know that the person you are living with cares for you and loves you," Azar said to Asim while they were watching TV that evening.

"Every wife cares for her husband. Our moms did, our grandmothers did," Asim said.

"No, my dear friend, times have changed. Women, no matter if they are Americans or Asians, are very independent, very self-centered now. I know this, my friend. Appreciate her." Azar had a kind of pain in his voice.

Whenever Safina saw Asim's friends or colleagues treating their wives with respect or talking about their accomplishments, she thought, *Will Asim be ever like that?*

February 2014, Southfield

Asim had started going back to work, but he was more worried than before about saving money. He sold the old Buick that Safina drove. "You can drop me and bring back the car; after all, my office is not too far. We spend a lot on two cars—insurance, gas, everything is so expensive these days," he said. He also stopped her monthly allowance of $200, saying, "You are earning money with your catering business."

Like always, Safina wanted to say something, but the fear of him disliking her made her scared and sad. She kept quiet and thought, *I am his responsibility, too. I am his wife.*

One day, when she overheard him talking to his mother on the phone, she became very depressed; she cried for hours after he left for work. As usual, he was complaining, asking why his mother did not find a highly educated girl for him who could bring home a big paycheck every month.

Why did his mother and sisters select me for Asim when they knew I was not the type of girl he wanted to get married to? Are all arranged marriages a disaster like ours? Are all husbands like mine? She thought about her dad; he always tried to respect her mom. Why not Asim?

After dinner one night, she gathered her courage and said, "I have researched a Montessori training course. It's an online course that is twelve months long, I will get a Montessori teacher diploma; then I can get a job at a local Montessori."

"You will study in the United States? Are you capable of it?" Asim couldn't have been more sarcastic.

"I am confident I can. They also offer help and English language courses through a local community college," Safina replied.

"How much will it cost?" he asked.

"$3,000."

"I don't have $3,000 to spend on your courses. I am not even sure if you can get a diploma or a job later on."

"I have collected $3,000. I will pay for it. Asim, please; I have never asked you for anything. Please don't say no, please." She was almost begging.

After a silent moment, he looked at her and said, "Okay, as long as I don't have to pay for it. But make sure you don't ignore the baby or the house. I have heard about this course because a colleague's daughter is doing it, so I doubt you will be able to complete it. According to my colleague, it's very difficult."

He is skeptical as usual, she thought. "I want to do it. I will work hard. I want to do something for myself, to achieve something. Thanks for saying I can try, Asim."

Safina was very happy for a long time. She enrolled herself in the course the following week. She worked hard day and night: she did all the housework in the morning, and then studied for few hours while the baby played or took a nap. She took help from few of her friends and went to the library with Anaya in the stroller to study. The course was very important to her. She wanted the diploma and a job as proof to the world that yes, Safina can also do it—she can reach for the sky.

March 2015, Southfield

"Asim, look! I got my diploma! It came in the mail." Safina showed it to him.

He looked somewhat happy. "I was not expecting it, but good. You managed to study in this country and get a diploma."

Safina was on cloud nine. She got a job at a local Montessori, and they gave her a discount on Anaya's fees too. Her monthly income would be almost $2,000, with overtime if she stayed after 3:30 p.m.

When she got her first paycheck after four weeks, she felt as if she had climbed Mount Everest or won the Miss Universe contest. She thought about depositing it in the bank but brought it home to show Asim first. She also

stopped at the mall and bought gifts for him and Anaya from the catering money she had saved.

"A twenty-three-hundred-dollar check made out to Safina Khan!" Asim exclaimed. He sounded excited.

"Yes. I did work some overtime too." She was beaming with pride.

"So what will you do with it?" he asked.

"I will lease a car. I think I can afford it, and it will be easier for both of us if we have two cars. Then I can save some money every month for down payment on a house, and I will also save money so on summer break we all can go for a vacation." Safina had thought about this quite a lot.

"You will not buy anything for yourself?"

"Maybe later I will buy a diamond ring. But first, a vacation to Disney World!" She felt like a little girl who got a magic wand.

Asim looked at her. He thought, *This woman who I have been insulting and humiliating for the last five years*

is thinking about helping me and taking us for a vacation? All of a sudden he realized that she had done so much for him: taken care of the house, the baby, even him when he fractured his leg. And she had earned a diploma and gotten a job! *But most of all, she has loved me. I have been so mean and insulting and she has never made a big deal about it. She does care about me, but isn't that what wives should do? And what are the responsibilities of husbands? I have never thought about taking her for a vacation and have never bought a gift for her; now she is ready to help me and support me? I have treated her so badly.*

Asim looked at her, and for the first time, she could sense some respect for her in his eyes.

"Safina, you have always taken care everyone and everything. You have been amazing," Asim said, his voice full of emotion.

"Oh, my dear, I have always loved you and will always do so!" She hugged him.

"Safina, I am grateful to God that I got you as my wife," he said.

She had waited so long to hear those words!

"I am too," she replied, tears rolling down her face.

They both stood there for some time, holding each other tightly. Maybe it was the sight of dollar bills which fascinated Asim, or maybe he finally did realize how lucky he was to have Safina as his wife—or maybe both—but for Safina, it was a feeling of accomplishment. She had finally conquered the battle of love and trust, perhaps the most important battle to conquer!

She was happy for herself and proud of her achievement. She was excited that she had attained financial stability and that they would eventually own property. She was also happy to see the warmth in her husband's attitude towards her.

Yes, she had overcome all the obstacles to attain her beautiful Amreeki Dream—a dream which was a reality now!